# bowery

## A horror story

MATTHEW VAUGHN

**Other Books By Matthew Vaughn:**

## Paperbacks:

The ADHD Vampire

Mother Fucking Black Skull of Death - Revised Edition

The Survivors

Hellsworld Hotel

30 Minutes or Less – The Complete Story

Stories from the Hellsworld Hotel

**The best deals on the E-books can be found at godless.com**

The Sexual Avenger Series on Godless

Lucifer's Mansion (A Hellsworld Hotel Prequel)

**Mephistophele's Den (A Hellsworld Hotel Prequel)**

**30 Minutes or Less**

**30 Minutes or Less Part 2**

**30 Minutes or Less Part 3**

**Rejects**

**Love Story**

**The Sexoricist**

**A Thanksgiving Story**

**The Magic Elf Christmas Massacre**

**Also :**

**The Classics Never Die! An Anthology of Old School Movie Monsters**

**Edited and Compiled by Edward and Matthew Vaughn**

**To Krystal, as always,**

**I couldn't do this**

**without you.**

# Table of Contents

# Chapter 1

The morning is cool, and the birds are out, chirping in full force. Out past the big wooden barn a thick fog is obscuring most of the farm. As George walks to the barn the dew-covered grass coats his work boots in a wet sheen. The sound of cows mooing, and pigs rutting, is so common to him anymore that they barely register. George just thinks about the tasks he has ahead of him as he grabs the handle of the barn door and pulls it towards him, the large hinges creaking in protest.

Inside the barn is something else he's grown accustomed to, the smell of shit in the air. Cow manure is ever present in the barn no matter how much you try to shovel it out, it's just a constant. George walks by the stalls holding all their livestock, some moo when they see him with the expectation that food is coming soon. Some haven't stirred from the night's slumber yet. George walks past them all, his goal to check on their newest heifer, brought in just last night.

George pulls the thick key ring from his pocket as he approaches the stall door. Stopping in front of the stall George lifts the lock and jams the key inside and twists. The thick master-lock pops open smoothly, and George pulls it out of the clasp and hangs it on a wooden slat to his right. The door swings open wide, and he steps into the stall and sees her. She's pretty big pregnant, it's the main reason she's here, and ready to be hooked up to the milking machine.

Her plump ass is facing George and as he walks up to her, he slaps her ass. It's a sharp sting against her bare skin.

"Come on bitch, time to wake up," George says in a thick country accent. His voice sounds rough, and mean, and the woman opens her eyes and is completely confused. Her vision is blurry from sleep and what she sees of her surroundings is unfamiliar and frightening. Her body feels sore, aching all over, and right away something isn't right. She tries to turn her head to look around, to see what he is doing, and in a panic realizes she can't move. Her head and shoulders are locked in between metal bars and her arms and legs are restrained.

"What the fuck is this?" she says, the terror creeping into her voice scaring her even more.

"Shut the fuck up bitch, cows don't talk," George says with his back to her. He pulls two plastic cups connected to long tubes from their hooks on the wall. He turns to her and sees her face, her big, frightened eyes staring up at him. She's very pretty, they don’t get many that look like her in this place. George doesn’t know and doesn't care that her name is Sandra. She's an expecting first-time mother, bordering on eight months pregnant. All George cares about is that she is on all fours, strapped to their milking table.

In the center of the table is a hole cut so that her huge belly hangs through.

At the front edge of the table, her engorged tits hang down, nipples pointing to the dirt floor. George crouches down, and holding the two tubes in one hand, he reaches his other under Sandra and fondles a dangling breast. He lifts it, then squeezes as she lets out a quick cry of pain.

"Help me, please, what's happening?" she asks and starts to cry. Tears are running down her face and landing on the dirt floor near George's feet. "Please, help me! Oh. God, what is happening? My baby, I can't feel my baby!"

"I've already told you to shut the fuck up," George says again, and this time he doesn't sound happy at all. She complies and quietly sniffs and whimpers. He squeezes and pulls on Sandra's tit, stopping to work her big, red, puffy nipples before squeezing and pulling some more. A few drops of milk begin to appear from her nipples and George nods. He takes one of the plastic cups and pushes it onto the breast he had been manhandling, then repeats the process on the other.

When George is satisfied that the cups are in place, he turns back to where the tubes connect to and turns a machine on. Simultaneously as when Sandra hears the whir of the machine begin, she feels the suction against her breasts. It's painful, they are sucked into the cups until they can't go any farther, and the feel of her already irritated nipples cramped into these devices is awful.

"Ow, it hurts, why are you doing this to me?" Sandra says, forgetting his last threatening remarks about not talking. She fights against her restraints, she desperately wants to be free to pull those things off of her tits, but it's a useless effort.

"You're a feisty little bitch, aren't you?" George says walking closer to her. She looks up at him through eyes blurred by tears and he reaches down and grabs a handful of her hair. "You're going to learn to keep your mouth shut. Cows don't fucking talk, they moo, or they don't say shit. We're going to break you though, don't you worry about that."

George yanks on her hair, which is agony

to Sandra when her head won't give to move with him. He lets go thankfully and walks around her out of her vision. She's crying, and inwardly hoping for some movement from her baby, her little boy she's been excited to meet for the past half a year after learning she was pregnant. A hand on her ass pulls her from inside of herself and she stiffens up. She feels him run his thick, calloused fingers down and in between her legs. She tries in vain to shake him off, to kick out her legs, something to make him stop. He spreads her lips and rubs between them. She's dry and his fingers, made hard and rough from years of hard work, hurt her. He pushes one of the fingers in and she winces, crying out.

"Oh, you've got a tight pussy, don't you?" He says. She feels him pull one of her ass cheeks and the cool morning air hits her exposed asshole. Her sphincter instinctively constricts. George pushes his big thumb against her tightened hole and Sandra tries and relax her sphincter to relieve herself of the pain. "Tight fucking asshole on you too."

Sandra is relieved when George pulls his fingers from her holes, even though a jagged fingernail cuts into her as he pulls free, causing her to cry out in pain. He's still behind her, she can hear him rustling around doing something, but she can't turn to look to see what's happening.

"They say sexual stimulation helps the milk production, gets it really flowing," George says as his overalls hit the dirt floor at his feet. He has nothing on under them, and Sandra feels his hard cock as he pushes it in between her legs.

"No, no, no!" she says, crying even harder now and trying to shake her head, shake anything to free herself of this nightmare. George reaches down and spreads her labia with one hand and pushes his cock into her dry hole. He's not gentle and rams it in without any thought to how it feels to Sandra. She screams, feeling like he ripped her open as he shoved himself inside. There's nothing she can do but sit there and take it as he repeatedly slams his cock in and out of her. She's crying and pleading while he grunts and digs his fingers into the soft flesh of her ass cheeks.

"I don't hear any mooing bitch!" he says in between his grunts. As he thrusts into her, her stomach pushes harder against the cutouts of the table she's strapped to, the edge of the wood digging into her belly. "Come on bitch, moo for me, moo for me so I can cum."

In all of her blinding pain, her thoughts swirling with concern for her baby, what's happening to her affecting him, this man forcing himself into her, no condom, the possibility of disease. Even with all that she had quickly running around inside her head, she refused, absolutely would not moo for this piece of shit rapist.

His fingers tightened and dig deep into her flesh. She can feel him release into her and it makes her nauseous. He pumps slowly a couple more times before he finally pulls out. She feels relieved and dirty and violated. She is sick to her stomach.

George pulls up his overalls and walks around in front of Sandra. She can see his disgusting cock dangling near her face, dripping with his semen. She closes her eyes as he grabs her hair again and uses it to wipe off his dick.

“That's fine bitch, you will moo for me. I’m going to fucking break you, just like I've broken all these other heifers in here,” he says with a laugh.

Sandra can’t help herself then, her stomach heaves and she gags and dry heaves. The table digs into her flesh as she heaves a couple of times before she finally pukes a chunky, brown sludge from deep inside her. She coughs and gags as it drips from her lips. George just laughs as the putrid vomit hits the dirt and splashes on his boots. Once he hooks his overalls back in place, George turns and leaves the stall, leaving Sandra to continue pumping milk as her body is racked with sobs.

# Chapter 2

"Lookee there boys, you tell me that isn't a fine-looking heifer," George says, loud and proud. Next to him is another older, country-grown man by the name of Steph, and a much younger, sullen-looking boy that goes by Shitheel. They had been teasing the boy, torturing him really, and calling him Shitheel for so long that he doubted anyone remembered what his actual name was.

Sandra hadn't even realized she had fallen asleep, still tied up like livestock, until the voices pulled her from a dreamless sleep. She couldn't believe that with what was happening to her she could just fall asleep like that, but she did, her tits still connected to the pumping machine, her pussy raw and sore.

"Got damn George, she's about the prettiest bitch I've ever seen," Steph says. He hocks out a big wad of tobacco spit onto the dirt floor at their feet. "What about you Shitheel, what do you think of that?" he says, slapping Shitheel on the chest, knocking the wind out of the boy.

The men were standing behind Sandra so she couldn't turn her head at all to look behind her. She just stared down at the dirt floor, at the drying puke on the ground, exposed with her naked ass and pussy on display for these sick men. She wants to ask them to let her go, to beg them to please not hurt her or her baby anymore. But she's afraid of what they might do to her.

"Uh, yeah, she's a beaut," Shitheel says, rubbing his chest where Steph hit him. He spoke with hesitation; he did think that Sandra was good-looking. Bent over with her sex on display like that, who wouldn't be turned on? But Shitheel isn't like the rest of the farmers there, he did not revel in raping and torturing the livestock.

"You say that like you don't mean it?" George says walking around to Sandra's head. She couldn't bring herself to look up at the rapist piece of shit. He walks over to the milking machine to check its progress. "You don't like the females, boy? You prefer the bulls, you want a big fat cock to suck on instead?"

George and Steph both laugh.

"Wha? No, that's not what I'm saying," Shitheel says in sad defense of himself.

Steph walks up behind Sandra, and she jumps at the feel of his hand on her bare skin. He pulls her ass cheeks apart and she inwardly cringes, silently repeating no over and over. She can't go through that again, that violation, what is all of this doing to her baby? She feels so helpless and weak, she should be protecting her baby until he's born, but instead, she's letting him down.

"Look at that asshole," Steph says. He leans down and puts his nose close to her anus and inhales deeply. "Oh yeah, that is nice. She ain't shit yet at all?"

"Nope, not yet," George says not turning around from his work.

Steph gets in close and runs his tongue up Sandra's ass crack, from her taint to her asshole, staying right there and licking her hole a couple of times. Sandra tightens up and whimpers at the sensation.

"I like it better after they shit, I like getting that little tang from the shit on my tongue," Steph says, standing up and looking at Shitheel. "You'd probably rather drink some thick semen from a fucking bull stud though wouldn't ya faggot?"

Shitheel turns his head away, his face burning from anger. He hates these men, the way they constantly treat him, talking down to him, calling him names. He hears Steph's overalls rustling and knows what the old man is doing, he's had to witness it so many times before.

George turns to Sandra and leans down next to her face.

"Looks like you're about dried up for now," he says. She has her eyes on him, trying to ignore what is happening behind her. George is looking at her face the moment Steph pushes his fat cock against her asshole and registers the pain and agony as she squeezes her eyes shut and the tears start rolling down her cheeks. She cries out at the feeling of her asshole tearing as Steph pushes his swollen head past her ring. “Come on bitch, moo for me.”

George watches her for a moment, her pain and discomfort making him hard again. He reaches under her and goes to grab one of the plastic cups suctioned to her tit. Her breasts are swinging as they hang under her from Steph fucking her in her ass. George is annoyed by this, but he doesn’t say anything as he grabs one of her swinging tits finally and pulls the cup off, then the other. He stands up and turns from her to put the cups and tubes back on their hooks near the machine. He turns back and watches Steph as he grunts while slamming into her repeatedly. It only lasts a few seconds more before the farmer lets out one final grunt and cums. He pulls out of Sandra with no regard for her and she whimpers.

“Ew yeah, you liked that didn’t ya?” Steph

says as he slaps her across one cheek, the sting causing her to tense her whole body up. "She was so tight, felt like I was the first ever been up her that way."

Steph laughs as he looks over to Shitheel, who is walking up to Sandra and helping George prepare to unlock her from her bonds. Shitheel grew up working on the farm, he knows what to do instinctively. When the milking is finished, the cows are unlocked and led to their stall until they're ready to be milked again. George has his big key ring out and is unlocking the bars that held Sandra's head in place.

Sandra isn't sure what is happening exactly. She can tell they are pulling the bars and straps off of her, but she knew they couldn't be letting her go. She lay there on the milking table, unsure of what to do. She can feel the one man's hot semen running out of her ass hole and down her crack and it is all she can focus on. After the bars holding her head in place are removed, she moves her stiff neck around. She is sore and has a crick in the right side, but it feels good to be able to move her head around. There is still a leather collar around her neck and George fastens a leash to it. He pulls and she moves to rise from the table, her legs wobbly but she tries to stand. Something sharp and stinging hits her in the lower back, just above her ass and she cries out and falls back down onto her hands and knees.

"Cows can't fucking stand bitch," George said, Sandra looks over and through her tear-blurred vision she sees the whip in his free hand, the other is holding her leash. She doesn't say anything, just complies and lifts her big belly from the table and climbs down next to it, her knees and palms digging into the rough dirt floor. George starts walking, leading Sandra out of that stall. She holds her head down as they pass Steph and Shitheel. She feels humiliated by their treatment and can't bear to look at them.

George leads her down a length of stalls similar to the one she had been in. She turns to look and sees other women in these stalls, their eyes looking empty as they look at her with a dead stare. She wonders how long they had been here. She had just been raped twice and hooked to a machine that milked her, in just one day, and she already feels like her spirit is broken. Have the women here been living with these men doing this to them repeatedly? She didn't think she could last being treated like this much longer.

She is led into an open stall with a pile of hay in one corner. George unleashes her without saying a word and turns and leaves, closing the stall door behind him.

# Chapter 3

Sandra lay curled up into a ball, her arms wrapped around her belly like she is trying to protect it, trying to block out the sounds that come in all around her. She can feel the baby move inside her and that brings her a lot of comfort. She worries about the trauma those men have put her body through and how it will affect the baby. She worries about what is going to happen once the baby comes. How can she deliver a baby in here? Who is going to deliver it, one of those rapists? She has no idea where she is, how is anyone going to find her to rescue her? Seeing those other women, that broke Sandra. If they are here too, that means that no one knows about this place and what is going on in it. She's never getting rescued. She starts crying again, letting the tears roll down her cheeks into the rough hay that is beneath her.

The stall door swings open and Sandra flinches away, afraid it's going to be one of them again. Shitheel comes into her stall, and she relaxes a little. He is the only one that didn't rape her earlier. That doesn't mean he's a good guy, but at that moment she is less scared of him than the other two. It helps that he is so young too, he gives off an air of innocence.

"Here's some food," Shitheel says, setting a metal container down in front of Sandra. She ignores it and sits up. Her naked breasts swing loosely as she moves, and she covers them in shame.

"Help me, please," she says to him, her voice low. He looks at her and she can't tell if it's a look of pity or lust. "I'm worried about my baby, I need to get out of here, I need to see a doctor. Please help me."

Shitheel just stands there looking at her

and Sandra starts to recoil from his eyes.

"You better eat, for your strength," he says and turns abruptly and walks out, slamming the stall door closed behind him. Sandra sits there, staring at the stall door. She hears a woman crying out in pain somewhere out past that door. A couple of women moo. They actually fucking moo.

She looks down into the contents of the metal tray that Shitheel brought in and is at once repulsed. It looks like ground hamburger that hasn't been cooked completely. It's slimy and smells like it could be spoiled. How can they expect her to eat that? If it's uncooked it could hurt the baby. She scoots away from it and moves to a new area on her hay, wincing at the pain coming from her probably torn asshole. She sees there's blood on the hay where she had been sitting and she starts crying again. She's never felt so hopeless in her entire life.

Sandra's body, tired from the abuse and growing a tiny human inside of it succumbs to sleep. Her sleep is rough and fitful, full of nightmares. When she wakes, she is confused by the dreams she doesn't remember and waking in a strange place. She hears a baby crying and her first thought is to grab her belly as she wonders if it's her baby crying. Remnants and flashes of her nightmares worsens her confusion. She feels her big round belly with all its stretch marks and is a little relieved at least. But a baby is crying somewhere, and now she notices a woman, also crying. She slowly stands up as she tries to pinpoint exactly where the sounds are coming from.

At the back of her stall, Sandra wiggles a bare toe in between two boards and lifts herself to look around. There's not much to see in the small amount of time she's up before her weight makes it impossible for her to keep herself up. She decides to try the other side of her stall.

"Hey," a voice says in a low harsh whisper. "Hey, stop."

Sandra looks around, at first, she thinks there's something in her stall with her. A talking mouse? She must be going crazy already thinking like this. Then it hits her, there's someone in the stall next to her. She walks close to the wall and lowers her heavy belly down as she crouches and looks through one of the gaps in the slats. There's a woman, naked and dirty, her hair looks like it hasn't been combed in months.

"Hello?" Sandra says to the woman.

"You better stay down on your hands and knees. Don't let them see you standing up," the voice says.

"I'm Sandra," Sandra tells the woman. "Who are you?"

"I'm a cow, cows don't have names," the woman says. Sandra realizes the woman is on her hands and knees and she can see her dip her head down like she's drinking from a bucket or something. "You're a cow too, you don't have a name either."

"I'm not a cow, I have a name. I told you my name is Sandra," she said, gripping the slats that made her stall wall. "You aren't a cow either."

"Better be quiet, cows don't talk," the woman said, she talked in an almost bored way like there was something else she could be doing with her time.

"I'm not a cow!" Sandra says, her voice becoming louder. There is a sound outside of her stall and the woman next to her looks up, then turns away. The door to Sandra's stall flies open and George is there.

"What the fuck is going on in here?" he speaks. He's wearing an apron that is covered in dark red blood, with thick, rubber gloves that reach his elbows. Sandra's first thought is he looks like someone straight out of a horror movie. "I heard you talking, cows don't fucking talk!"

He shouts at her as he walks into the stall, pulling his thick gloves off. Sandra falls onto her ass, it's already sore and she lets out a yelp as he towers over her. George kicks out with one of his large work boots and it catches her on her tailbone, the pain is unreal. She grabs at her ass as she screams out and he kicks her again. She gets it in the ass again, but her hand is there, and her fingers get the brunt of the blow.

"Oh god, please stop!" Sandra is crying.

"I'm sorry, I'm sorry!"

Her eyes are closed so she doesn't see George's big fist as it comes down on her. He smashes it into her face and her nose explodes with pain and warmth.

"Cows don't talk! They moo!" George screams at her. He hits her again, this time more on the top of the head as she's cradling her battered face. She doesn't even register the blow, she's so dazed, everything is swimming around her. His voice is unintelligible and sounds like syrup. "You're gonna moo for me bitch. You're gonna moo."

At some point, the world quit spinning around Sandra, and she can focus again. She sees that George is gone; she has no idea how much time has passed. Her face hurts, her hand hurts and she has a headache. She touches her swollen belly as she feels a kick from the inside. At least the baby is still okay, that is the only comfort she has right now.

# Chapter 4

Sandra is on the milking machine again. Her face is sore, she can feel the puffiness under her eyes and as much as her nose still hurts, she doesn't think it is broken. She's not so sure about the fingers on her hand though. Her left hand is swollen, three of her fingers look like little sausages they're swollen so badly. Being led by leash out of her stall and into the milking stall was torture, but she grit her teeth and took it.

Climbing up onto the table wasn't much easier, and as George strapped her down, every movement caused her wounds to throb. But, once in place, everything did calm down some. At least laying on the table, her big belly hanging through the hole, she can take the pressure off of her hand and fingers.

"She sure isn't as pretty today," Steph says standing in front of her. "Was you trying to knock her teeth out, so she'd suck your pecker without biting it off?"

Steph laughs and Sandra cringes inwardly. She couldn't imagine one of these dirty farmers putting their cocks in her mouth and how bad they might smell and taste.

"I don't have to knock her teeth out to get my dicked sucked. If I wanted this cow to suck it then she would suck it," George says. She can see him, his back is to her, and she knows he is getting the plastic cups with the tubes for milking her. She's not excited at all about having those things suctioned to her breasts again. She hears something behind her and can see Steph looking at something behind her. She immediately tenses up expecting the worst.

"You get that meat ground up Shitheel?" Steph asks.

"Yes sir," Shitheel says in his quiet manner. Sandra watches Steph walk around her and worries about him being behind her.

"You looking at that pretty ass, boy? You want to put your little pecker in it?" Steph says. She jumps at his touch. His big, calloused thumb slides in between her cheeks and rubs her sore sphincter. "Yeah, this one likes it in the ass, like a good cow whore. Your little pecker probably wouldn't do much though."

The thumb disappears, and Sandra is relieved, but she expects it to be replaced by something bigger and that scares her.

"She's lucky I done fucked that brown cow just a little bit ago, drained my balls in that bitch good. But I might swing back through here after lunch, depends on what I got going on," Steph says and slaps her hard on this ass. She winces, it stings her skin, her ass is still hurting from George's beating. She feels like shit between the beating and rapes and lack of food. She isn't sure how she can survive like this, but she has to, for her baby.

George turns to her with the milking cups and kneels in front of her. She can see his face better today; she's not blinded by panic and confusion like she was the day before. He's older and ugly. His face is weather-beaten, and his hair is buzzed short. He smiles at her with yellow and brown teeth. She can smell the cigarette smoke on him. He holds the cups in one hand and with his free one reaches under her and grabs one of her hanging breasts and runs his hands down it as he squeezes. It hurts and Sandra winces but doesn't say anything.

"That's a good cow," he says to her as he works on her puffy nipple until milk begins to drip. He takes one of the cups and fastens it to her breast before adjusting himself and working the second breast.

In no time Sandra is hooked up with the suction pulling on her nipples and the skin of her breasts. It is uncomfortable and she hates it. George walks away from her, towards her ass where Steph and Shitheel are standing.

"Get her some feed, she didn't eat

anything last night and she needs to keep her strength up to keep producing," George says. Shitheel nods and exits the stall. Sandra tries to listen to what George and Steph talk about but they're talking low, and the milking machine is running so she can't make it out.

Shitheel comes back and walks into view holding another metal tray. She watches him as he grabs a bucket from over in the corner, flips it upside down, and places it on the ground under her face. He sets the metal tray down onto the overturned bucket and Sandra sees it's the same ground meat as before. It looks shiny and barely cooked, there's juices in it that look like blood and Sandra's stomach does a flip.

"You better eat it, they don't like it when you don't eat," Shitheel says to her. She looks up at him, just a skinny, dirty kid. He seems harmless even though he works at this fucked up place too, but he is different than the other two.

Someone shoves her head down from behind, pushing her face into the disgusting meat.

"Eat up you fucking cow," George says,

holding her head down as she fights against him. His big hand is heavy on the back of her head, there's nothing she can do to push it away. She tries to frantically move her head back and forth, but the meat just goes in her nose, and some gets into her mouth, it doesn't taste awful so much as it's just bland. She finally surrenders. stops fighting, and sucks some of it into her mouth, and reluctantly chews.

"There we go you little bitch. We need you to keep your strength, we need you to keep pumping out that milk," George says. He relaxes his hold on her head but keeps his hand there, patting her head and rubbing it like she is some kind of animal.

As Sandra swallows the meat down her stomach groans in protest of it. She chews a mouthful and bites down on something hard, it feels like it might have cracked her tooth. She can feel it with her tongue, it's a tiny hard piece of something and she pushes it out of her mouth and tries to spit it out. She assumes it could be a piece of bone and she wonders, not for the first time, what this is she is eating. Finally, her stomach has had enough, she dry heaves, the food that's in her mouth falling half chewed back into the tray.

George laughs at her and she dry heaves again. His hand is still on the back of her head and it's limiting the amount of movement she has. She tries to move away from the tray of meat and starts vomiting. She can't move far enough away and some of it goes into the tray, covering the meat with bile and chunks of undigested food. Most of it lands under her though, in the dirt on the floor near where she threw up the day before. She tries to hold her head away from the tray of meat that now smells like vomit but is surprised to find George still hasn't removed his hand completely. He laughs again.

"Don't think you don't have to eat just because you had an accident," he says, and Sandra stiffens. "Come on bitch, get back to it. You need it now more than ever. Can't have you going out on us."

Sandra pushes against his hand again, but she's already lost this fight once. She still tries, not wanting anything to do with the nasty concoction of sick and half-cooked meat in front of her face. George isn't letting up though and she knows that she doesn't exactly have a choice. Sandra looks down at the mess in front of her, the slimy brown liquid from her vomit is starting to soak into the meat, and the chunks she puked up kind of blend in with the ground meat. It's the smell that she's having the most trouble with. She just wishes she could hold her nose at least.

Sandra finally gives in again, for the second time, and moves her face down into the disgusting mess in front of her. She scoops up the mixture of vomit and meat into her mouth and begins to chew. When she tries to swallow it, she immediately gags and worries it isn't going down.

"You better not puke it up again. I will hold you down and force this into you," George says. Sandra somehow manages to keep it together and swallows the mess. A slimy lump slides down her throat. After that, she manages to eat without too much of an issue. George pats the back of her head.

"Good girl," he says, and she's relieved to finally feel his hand go away. As she eats, Sandra looks up to see Shitheel still standing there looking down at her. She feels embarrassed and insecure as she continues to lap meat up into her mouth.

"I like it when they struggle like that," Steph says. She feels a hand on her lower back, she has no idea whose it is, George or Steph, and she tries to ignore it and just concentrate on eating.

"Yeah, when they puke the first time it really gets me," George says. He unbuckles his overalls and lets them fall to the ground. Sandra hears this and closes her eyes shut tight. She keeps eating, pretending what is getting ready to happen isn't going to happen. "It's perfect timing for needing to stimulate milk production."

"One of these days we need to make that pussy Shitheel stimulate one of these bitches," Steph says as he watches George spit on his thick cock and rub the saliva around his swollen head and veiny shaft. "You need to pop your cherry on a female, boy. Quit fucking around with those bulls you're always sucking off."

George pushes his hard prick against Sandra, and she instinctively tightens up as tears begin to roll from her eyes. George just pushes harder, forcing himself into her again. She opens her mouth, half-chewed food falling out as she gasps in pain, the thickness of his dick ripping into her dry vagina. Sandra silently cries over her disgusting food as he fucks her, his cock moving in and out feeling like it is tearing her open. George grabs onto the flesh of her hips and digs his fingers in deep as he pounds into her with no regard for her comfort.

"I think she likes you, George!" Steph says as he whoops and hollers. Sandra feels a pop inside of her body and thinks about the baby. She wants to grab her belly, to comfort herself with the feeling that he's in there and safe, but with her hands restrained she can't do anything but sit there and take this abuse.

There's liquid running out of Sandra that she feels on her inner thighs. George looks down and sees the clear liquid squishing out of her around his cock.

"Look at that, she's cumming all over your dick!" Steph yells and laughs.

"No, I think the water just broke on this one," George says as he grunts and continues to pound into her. He doesn't stop as he looks up across from him. "Shitheel, go get the birthing stall ready. We're gonna be taking this one's calf in a little bit." Sandra opens her eyes at this news. She sees Shitheel nod and disappears from her view.

"My...my baby?" Sandra says and Steph runs up to her and slaps her on the side of her head. The blow hits her ear. causing a ringing sensation in her head.

"Shut the fuck up, cows don't talk! You can moo bitch, that's all you can do," Steph yells, spit flying from his lips onto Sandra's face. "Moo for George like you're having a good time. Moo for your master while he's fucking you bitch!"

Sandra's crying intensifies as George's grunting gets louder, his flesh is slapping against her flesh and the milking machine is whirring. Sandra's going into sensory overload as everything is assaulting her all at once. George's grip tightens on her flesh as he lets out a final grunt and she feels his seed spurting inside of her. He slides out as unceremoniously as he had slid in, and he wipes something off of his hand onto her ass cheek. She can feel the warm liquid oozing down her inner thighs and doesn't know if it's from him or her. She thinks about her baby, she's absolutely worried about what is happening to him, and what is going to happen to him.

"We'll leave her here milking for a while, she doesn't need to be delivered right away, she'll hold for a while," George says as he fixes his overalls back on in place.

"I need to check on that bitch that gave birth yesterday, see how she's holding up this morning," Steph says as he opens the stall door. "Got that brown cow too that needs to be hooked up in here before her milk dries up."

She can barely hear them as they chit-chat on their way out of the stall. She hangs her head in shame, pain, and fear. Sandra doesn't know how much more of this she can endure.

# Chapter 5

Sandra is lost inside her mind when the miking machine is turned off. She barely registers George pulling the cups from her tits and then latching the lease to her neck.

"Come on bitch, we have work to do, let's get moving," he says to her as he pulls on the leash. She looks up at him and obediently climbs down from the milking table. Her swollen hand and possibly broken fingers throb with pain. She registers the liquid still seeping down her inner thighs as she moves. She doesn't remember the last time she felt the baby move.

George leads her out of the stall, and she

sees Steph there, holding the leash of another woman who is naked and on all fours. She's dirty, her hair is all matted like it hasn't been combed in a very long time. Sandra notices the woman has loose, flabby skin hanging down from her stomach. The two women make eye contact, but the other one quickly adverts her eyes. George tugs on her leash, making her move on as Steph and the other woman head into the milking stall.

She takes in her surroundings as they go and realizes she is being taken in the opposite direction than the stall she slept in for the night. She refuses to think of it as her stall, she refuses to believe that she will stay here forever, like the woman she saw, or the one she talked to the night before. There is movement around her as they make their way to wherever George is leading her. She sees into stalls as they go, and she sees more women. *How many women do they have at this place?* She wonders to herself.

Her knees begin to hurt as they continue, she isn't used to crawling around all over the place like this. Her big, pregnant belly swings uncomfortably under her as she crawls. She just wants to stand up and walk, wouldn't that be better, faster, than what they are doing? She starts to slow down and George tugs on her and tells her to move it. Her knees and her palms hurt pretty bad; she has no idea how she'll be able to crawl all of the way back after this.

After what seems like an eternity, George stops in front of a door. When he pulls it open, she is blinded by a bright light. Something about this terrifies her, she feels like she's being led to her death.

"Come on bitch, I have more work to do today, I don't have time for you playing around," George says as he tugs on her collar. Sandra complies, she doesn't have much of a choice.

The inside resembles an operating room. The floor is not dirt and everything in it is stainless steel, giving off the appearance of being semi-sterile. Movement catches her eye, and she turns her head to see a man sitting in the corner.

He's dressed in overalls and work boots like George and Steph, and he's wearing dark glasses that remind her of welding goggles. He stands up from his chair and looks down at her.

"Here she is, what a fine specimen," the man, Leningrad, says.

"Up on the table," George says. Sandra turns from the man and looks at the shiny, metal table in the middle of the room. It is really low to the ground so that as George leads her to it, she can just climb up onto it while still on all fours.

"We're going to need you to lie down for this," Leningrad says. "On your back."

Sandra feels the desire to comment that she's never seen a cow lying on its back before, but she chooses not to, knowing it will result in her being beaten again. Instead, she complies. The steel is cold against her naked back and butt. George unhooks the leash from around her neck, but she feels him tugging on her collar still and when he's finished, she can barely move her head.

The two men walk around her naked body on the table, securing her arms and legs. When they are finished, they stand down at her feet and stare at her, she can barely see their heads over the top of her round belly.

George stays there while Leningrad walks away. Sandra can't see where he goes so, she just watches George, who stares at her without saying or doing anything. She hears what sounds like a squeaky wheel on her left and tries to turn her eyes enough to see what it is. Leningrad rolls an IV on a hook up next to her. She can see the liquid-filled bag swinging from its hook and terror overcomes her.

"Wha… what are you doing?" Sandra blurts out. Leningrad looks over at George.

"She's still talking?" he asks.

"We're still breaking this one in," George says, walking towards Sandra's head.

"Do I need to bring one of the bulls in to take over for you?" Leningrad says turning back to his work.

"No, no. Steph and I have this,' George says. He reaches down and grabs Sandra's chin, squeezing where she is bruised and swollen. "Listen cow, I better not hear anything except a moo from you. We've been gentle so far, if you try to talk again, we'll stop being gentle with you."

Sandra's eyes were wide with pain and terror. She said nothing, just stared at George, her eyes watering and tears running down her dirty face.

"It is still early I suppose. I won't report this, but you better step it up before one of the supervisors come around and catches her talking," Leningrad says as he jams a needle into her arm. Sandra winces from the jab. He hooks the small tube to her and reaches up to turn on the drip from her bag.

George holds Sandra's stare until he sees her eyes cloud over and knows the medication is working. He lets go of her face and walks around to where Leningrad is pulling a tray over with multiple surgical equipment. On the tray are two aprons and two pairs of thick, rubber gloves. Each of the men picks up an apron and puts them on over their heads and reaches behind them to tie them on, then picks up a pair of gloves and labor to pull them on. Once situated in their gear, Leningrad pulls the tray over so that it almost rests over the top of Sandra's naked form. She tries to look at them, but her eyes won't focus, the drugs have made it hard for her to pay attention to anything that is happening.

George looks over to Leningrad as he picks up a scalpel and brings it to Sandra's round belly. She feels the pressure as he pushes the scalpel into her lower stomach, right under her baby bump but just above her pubic area. It doesn’t hurt, it’s just a sensation to her. Blood sprays wildly from the incision as Leningrad cuts from one side of Sandra's belly to the other. George lays towels around the cut to catch the blood flowing as it runs down either side of her body and drips onto the floor.

Leningrad cuts into each layer of the abdominal wall and then the uterus. Once she has been opened up, Leningrad reaches inside Sandra, his hands feeling around her organs as he works. Sandra feels his presence inside of her, she feels herself being jostled as he digs around inside of her, moving organs to get to his prize.

Sandra goes in and out as the procedure continues. Her eyes roll up into her head and she falls out of consciousness, then she opens her eyes to find herself in the bright room but she can't concentrate on anything that is happening. She repeats this continuously, her mind is cloudy and murky, and everything has a dreamlike quality to it.

Leningrad pulls the baby from inside her, he is covered in a slimy substance, and he hands the tiny being to George who in turn sets it in the bucket on the tray. Leningrad immediately sets to work putting Sandra back together.

At one point a baby is crying, and this causes Sandra to start crying. Her body feels like it is floating over the table, hovering in the air just above it. Her belly feels unusually empty and hangs slack in the air.

Once Leningrad is satisfied with the work he has done and Sandra is sewn back together, he takes the cart with the screaming child and wheels it out of that room, disappearing into another.

# Chapter 6

For Sandra, time moves by in a cloudy daze where she can't differentiate between being awake or asleep. She lies on her pile of hay, she is given food, still the slimy, half-cooked slop in a tin pan. Her dreams are confusing and make no sense and leave her as quickly as they come. She feels very little pain and discomfort for having undergone surgery, or if she feels any she quickly forgets. Sandra has no sense of time, her life in her stall revolves around eating, sleeping, and shitting. She has no control over her transformation into the animal they want her to be. She barely exists mentally, her body just does what it needs to do to survive, and she is mostly unaware and blissfully ignorant of everything. Then, after an unknown amount of time passes, it is like she wakes up.

Sandra opens her eyes to the dullness of early morning. She hadn't realized before that there are windows in the ceiling, and she can tell the changes in the day. This place she is being held captive in is normally well-lit and camouflages the changes throughout the day. Looking up toward the ceiling Sandra can see big lights like what you would find in a warehouse, they are lifeless. She can see things about the ceiling she has never noticed before or hasn't bothered to see before.

Sitting up on her sparse pile of hay, straw stabbing the naked flesh of her ass, Sandra’s stomach is tight and sore. She looks down at the flabby skin that she last remembered as being tight and round while it held her baby. Where is her baby now? She has no memory of anything after being taken to the bright room and strapped to the table. There are faint thoughts of a baby’s cries, but she doesn’t know if that was just dreams or real memories. She grabs the thick flab of flesh in her hand and feels it, lifts it, and feels a slight irritation under it. She can lift it and see the incision that was made to cut her baby out of her.

Sandra looks up as George unlocks the stall door. He pulls the door open and sees her sitting there on her hay pile. He has a leash in his hands, and she gazes up at him as he walks toward her. She wants to ask about her baby, she wants to know what the hell is going on. But she is scared of the man and what he may do to her.

George snaps the leash onto her collar without uttering a word. He pulls on her tether letting her know she is to get on her hands and knees. Sandra obliges, noticing her hand doesn't hurt nearly as bad as it had before. The swelling is gone but her index and middle fingers are crooked, pointing in directions they had not her entire life. She tries to put it out of her mind as George leads her out of the stall. They turn right, in the opposite direction of the milking stall. As she crawls along the ground Sandra can see another woman far ahead of her being led by another man in overalls similar to George's. As they go, they pass empty stall after empty stall. She wonders if they're being led to something, and her first thought is to their deaths. She doubts that though. She has seen the dead eyes of women in there, she has seen the dirty women with matted hair, and knows that women stay here for a long time.

She sees the big open doors in front of her and can hardly believe it. George leads her outside, the bright, blinding sun causing her to lose her vision for a moment. It's cool out and goosebumps immediately dot her flesh all over her body. the grass is wet under her hands and knees, and as her vision returns, she sees that it's a field. Sandra gasps at the number of women in front of her. There might be a hundred women, naked, on their hands and knees, roaming around this huge, open field. She sees some with big pregnant bellies hanging under them and thinks again about her baby.

George scratches himself through his overalls before bending down and unlatching the leash from around Sandra's collar. He turns and slaps her hard on her ass.

"Get, enjoy your free time in the sun. You'll be milking again later," he says before walking away. She turns her head and watches as he goes back into the barn.

All around her women are lowering their heads and pulling up the grass with their teeth, chewing on the blades like they're cows. In front of her, she watches a pregnant blonde woman, her long hair hanging on either side of her head like two rat's nests. A dark brown liquid runs down her inner thighs as she just shits herself right there without any reaction. Sandra backs away from her and bumps into someone. She turns around and sees the woman from the stall next to her. The woman makes eye contact with her, and Sandra opens her mouth to speak and the woman shakes her head no. She turns and starts crawling away from Sandra.

Sandra crawls around the field, unsure of what to do with herself. She avoids piles of shit from some women that defecated big dark turds in the grass. She refuses to try and eat the grass; she doesn't understand why these women are eating it. She enjoys the feel of it, though her knees are turning green, and her fingers are hurting more and more the longer she crawls around. She sees a little commotion to her left and since she has nothing else to do, crawls toward the women to be nosy.

A man is walking through the herd of women, he's huge and shirtless, with rippling muscles. In different circumstances, Sandra might have found him attractive. His eyes look dark, and he looks around like he's wandering aimlessly, his eyes not focusing on anything. The women all crawl away from the man as he walks around them. Sandra doesn't know what to do with herself she is glued to her spot, mesmerized by this monster of a man wandering around. He stops abruptly like something she can't see has grabbed his attention. He pushes his pants down exposing the biggest cock Sandra has ever seen before in her life. Its thickness looks unnatural like it's a prosthetic applied for a movie. The thing is rock hard, the purple head swelled to the point it looks like it might pop.

As Sandra continues to watch, the man turns and grabs the nearest woman. His selection of the woman seems arbitrary like he randomly grabbed the nearest body not caring who or what it was. The woman begins to struggle, a noise comes from her mouth like nothing Sandra has ever heard before. The man pushes his cock into the woman and Sandra does not think that it can possibly fit, there is just no way. The woman under him is trying to crawl away, her hands digging at the ground, grabbing at the blades of grass that just easily rip from the loose dirt. The man continues to push his massive cock against her, his shaft bending into an uncomfortable U shape between him and her. His fingers dig into the woman's flesh as she fights to get away, and little drips of blood appear at his fingertips as his nails pierce her flesh.

Finally, Sandra can see the women's pussy lip's part around his engorged bell end as it starts to enter her. Then she sees the women's flesh rip in between her pussy and her ass hole as more of the man's cock slides in. The woman is bucking and flailing, her weird noises turning into screams of pain and the man begins to fuck her, hard. There's blood flowing down and covering his cock as he penetrates her over and over. He's like a savage beast, horny and wild as saliva drools from his lips. The woman has all but given up now as he smashes her face and upper body into the ground. He practically stands on top of her, it looks like something that could be out of a porno if it wasn't rape and she wasn't bleeding. Sandra can't turn her eyes away from the ordeal, but she's sure this image will haunt her for a long, long time.

After what seems like forever but is more likely just minutes, the big man pulls out of the woman's ruined pussy. His cock is covered in red, its tip dripping with thick ropes of cum. He pulls his pants up, barely covering his still-engorged cock, and turns away from his conquest. The man stops as he sees Sandra sitting there watching. A sickening dread fills her and for a moment she believes she is going to throw up. The man takes a step toward her, fear paralyzing her even though she knows with every ounce of her being that she needs to run.

"Oh for fucks sake!" Steph calls out from behind her. She watches the man look up past her in recognition. "One of the fucking bulls got out!"

The muscular man looks back down at Sandra, she sees the tip of his cock poking up out of the top of his pants. The man's muscles ripple through his body as a thick blob of cum escapes from the head of his cock. He turns and runs away from her.

Steph and two men Sandra has never seen before appear on her right. They walk over to the woman lying motionless on the ground. Steph looks up from her lifeless body to the back of the man running away.

"Someone needs to check the pens and see how he got out, make sure all the others are still secure," Steph says to no one in particular. He turns back to the body of the woman. "Get her to the Doc to check her out."

The two men with Steph nod and grunt as they reach down and grab the woman under her armpits and at her knees. When they hoist her dead weight into the air blood splats from between her legs onto the grass. Steph pulls his ball cap off his head and runs a hand over his close-cropped scalp.

"Fuck, the supervisors are going to be pissed about this," he says and looks around at the herd of women. Just about all of them are minding their own business as if nothing has happened. Steph sees Sandra watching and smiles. He walks over to her and puts a hand on her face, rubbing across her nose and cheek and pushing a finger in her mouth. He tastes dirty and she can smell an odor that reminds her of spoiled milk.

"Well, well. Glad to see you up and moving around. Guess I'll be seeing you for milking later on."

He pulls his hand away and walks past her, following the men carrying the woman back into the barn.

# Chapter 7

When grazing time is over and all of the women are being led back into the barn, George pulls Sandra past her stall and down to the milking stall. The muscles of her stomach burn with pain. Sandra found herself looking forward to laying on the table while she was milked, it would give her body a chance to rest for a while, until George or Steph started raping her anyway. Once inside the stall, Sandra climbs up onto the table obediently while George shuts the stall closed behind them. Sandra's instantly relieved to be off of her hands and knees. They both sting from being rubbed raw on the ground.

George goes through the motions chaining

Sandra down and starts the milking process. Once she's incapacitated, she watches in horror as George pulls down his overalls. She knew it would be coming, but that still didn't prepare her for it actually happening.

"We need to get you bred so that you continue to produce milk," he says as he walks towards the back of her, leaving her eyesight. "Believe me, you want me to get you pregnant and not one of the bulls. You saw what happened today, they can get a little rough with you heifers."

Sandra squeezes her eyes shut, waiting for the inevitable. The door to the stall swings open and George turns to see Steph step inside.

"Aw George, I hate to interrupt," Steph says, his eyes going from Sandra's ass on display to George's hard pecker. "But that bull that got loose, they were trying to coral him back into the pens and he went nuts. He killed Jerrod."

"Jesus Christ," George says and pulls his overalls back up. "The supervisors know yet?"

"That's the only reason I came in here,

they do, and it's all hands-on deck," Steph says, his eyes roaming over Sandra's bare flesh again. "Otherwise, I wouldn't have interrupted you at work."

"Fucking hell, you seen Shitheel?"

"Not since we brought all the cows in from grazing," Steph says. To Sandra, the men's voices are getting quieter as they leave the stall.

She is trapped again, restrained to a table, completely helpless. She hates being exposed like this; it is an awful feeling. She stares at the ground with nothing to do but wait for them to come back. Wait for them to begin raping her again. She needs to get out of this place, she can't live like this. If she can't get out of there and find her baby what else was there for her? She might as well just kill herself rather than let one of these sick perverts knock her up. Or worse, have one of those bulls get a hold of her. The image of it raping that woman, how it ripped up her pussy as it fucked her. She shutters, her flesh breaking out in goosebumps.

The stall door opens up behind her and she

can feel someone walking in. Sandra tries to turn her head and see who it is, but it doesn't do any good. She has to wait for them to walk in front of her.

"I brought you lunch," Shitheel says as he leans down and slides a pan of the usual slimy, nasty-looking meat in front of her. Flies buzz around it, landing on the meat for a few seconds and then flying off. Sandra looks up at him.

"It's okay, go ahead and eat. I'm not like the others, I won't touch you," he says and sits in front of her, his legs crisscrossing in front of him. Sandra leans her head down and takes some of the meat into her mouth, she gags, still not used to the taste, but she manages to force it down without vomiting it back up.

"You know, I was meant to be a bull," he says. She eyes him while she eats, not sure if she should respond or refrain from talking so as not to get beat. "The mother cow produces all the bulls, she's not like you, her offspring are different. I don't know why she is the way she is, why the bulls come out as they do."

Sandra stops eating and is listening to Shitheel.

"Why...why aren't you a bull then?" she asks, taking a chance by talking to him.

"I was a runt. Look at me, do I look like that thing that was running around outside earlier?" He says, picking at hay lying in the dirt. "They were probably going to just get rid of me like they do the rest of the calves, but someone decided to spare me."

"They get...rid of the, uh, calves?" Sandra asks, her voice shaking.

"Yeah, they don't want anything here they can't use. They keep you pregnant, so you produce milk, but what are they going to do with a bunch of babies?" Shitheel looks at her. "I'm not supposed to let you talk you know."

Sandra wants to ask more about the babies, about her baby, but she shuts up, afraid of what might happen.

"I kind of like you though, I don't know why," he turns away and looks back at the milking machine. "I'm not like the others; I don't care if you talk. They'll beat you and rape you, but not me. Besides, I'm done with this place, I'm going to burn it all down."

"You're going to burn this place down?" Sandra asks hesitantly. Shitheel turns back to her, his face deadly serious.

"Yes. I let the bull free to cause chaos and confusion. And now, I'm going to burn this place." Shitheel stands up abruptly.

"What about me, what about the other women here," she watches him as he walks over to the milking machine. "What about the babies, my baby?"

The milking machine clicks off and the low hum dies away. Shitheel turns to her and begins to unstrap her bonds.

"I'm going to let you go, like I said, I like you. Do what you want to try to save the other cows, I don't care. If I were you, I'd just get the hell out of here and forget about the rest."

Once Sandra is free she stands up from the table, her leg muscles scream in protest and her stomach burns.

"What about the babies, my baby? Is there

still a chance for him?"

Shitheel stops as he moves toward the stall door. He turns and looks at her with a quizzical look on his face.

"No, there's no chance. What do you think we've been feeding you?" He glances down toward the pan on the ground she had just been eating out of, then he pulls the stall open and leaves.

Sandra looks at the aluminum pan and the slimy meat still at the bottom of it. Her world begins to spin, and she puts out a hand to stop herself from falling.

"No no no no no," she says as her hand touches the table but is unable to support her. She falls onto her bruised and swollen knees in the dirt and begins to retch. Everything she's just eaten, the remains of her baby, come vomiting out of her with an unrelenting force. She bends forward as she heaves, throwing a hand down to the ground to stop herself from face-planting. Her hands land in the thick bile and undigested meat in front of her. She continues to expel all the contents of her stomach into the dirt, her eyes pouring tears, streaming down her dirty face.

There's a lull in her getting sick and she leans over and grabs the aluminum pan, turning it over and dumping the contents into her lap. She cries out, her face turned upward, as she squishes the slimy meat in between her fingers and rubs it across her naked body. When she drags a hand across her still healing scar on her stomach it sends a searing pain through her body, but she ignores it. Sandra spreads apart her pussy lips with one hand and begins to stuff cold, slimy handfuls of meat up into herself. She scraps everything off of her naked flesh and proceeds to shove it into her cunt, taking two fingers and pushing it in as far as she can. When she's cleaned herself off, she reaches forward and scoops up the undigested meat in her puddle of vomit, thick ropes of bile stringing from her hand. She pushes this inside of her, her face a contorted, crying mess the entire time.

Once Sandra shoves as much ground remains of her baby up into herself, she pulls herself to her feet. Wiping at her wet mouth and cheeks with the back of her hands, Sandra looks around for a weapon. She wants to make them pay. George, Steph, anyone that played a part in the death of her baby. But the milking stall holds nothing in the way of weapons.

Sandra moves to the stall door and peers out. She doesn't see anyone around and slips out of the stall, her head turning back and forth constantly on the lookout as she walks quickly.

"Moo," a woman says as she walks by stalls. Every stall she passes has a woman inside, mooing and watching her walk by.

"Moo, wait!" a voice says, and Sandra stops to look. "Moo! Help me, get me out of here."

Sandra feels for the women trapped in this place, undergoing the abuse she too faced. If Shitheel actually burns the place down, all of these women locked in their stalls will surely die. She grabs the padlock on the outside of the stall door.

"It's locked, I'll have to find a key," Sandra says to the woman.

"Please, I don't want to be a cow anymore. Moo," the woman says, still on all fours, her face pressing against the stall door.

Sandra nods at the woman and turns away from the stall. She continues, quickly making her way through the place, constantly on the lookout for George or someone else working there. Turning a corner, she finds herself face to face with the door to the room where they took her baby from her. She has no desire to go in there again, just seeing the door breaks her down inside and she forces herself to keep it together and not fall apart now.

Sandra backs away from the door and moves on past it, wondering where the keys are and how in the world, she can possibly get them and rescue any of the women from this awful place.

# Chapter 8

Down a little way from the delivery room, Sandra finds another door. She tries the knob and it’s unlocked. She takes deep breaths, knowing that this could be a big mistake, but finally she twists the knob and pulls the door open. Inside it's filled with the hum of machines, reminding her of the milking machine she had been hooked up to. It's dark, the only light emanating from a back room. Sandra makes her way slowly, the floor under her bare feet cool, it's like vinyl or linoleum, definitely not the dirt floor where she came from.

At the edge of the backroom, Sandra listens. She can hear someone breathing in there, it's loud like they're asleep. The whir of the machines is louder, and there's a rancid odor wafting out. Sandra peeks around the corner and her mouth drops open.

The huge monstrosity in the room is the most obese woman Sandra has ever seen. Her rolls of fat cascade down her body in layers upon layers of doughy flesh. There is no definition of limbs or neck on the woman, she is literally just a huge blob. She is naked, one massive tit has a clear plastic cup attached to it that Sandra knows all too well is for milking. The other tit has a naked man attached to it. He's older, his skin is wrinkled and sagging off his body. The man is sitting in the folds of the woman's fat and has his lip suctioned to the big woman's breast, his hands wrapped around the large mammary and massaging the swollen flesh as he sucks.

Tubes are running into each of the fat woman's orifices. A thick accordion-style tube is in her mouth, its diameter is so big that the large woman's mouth is stretched open to an uncomfortable size. Sandra sees another tube just as big disappearing into the folds of her stomach that are hanging down and lying on her lap. A third tube disappears behind the woman, and Sandra can only assume these are feeding the woman and taking care of any waste she creates so that she doesn't have to be moved. She imagines moving the woman would be an enormous undertaking. Sandra follows the tubes away from the woman as they travel along the ceiling into a dark corner where tiny lights blink and she knows where the machine's whirl is coming from.

Sandra is fixed to her spot on the floor, she cannot force herself to look away from whatever is happening in the room. She instantly recognizes the man suckling the woman's teat, it's the doctor that took her baby from her. As she stands there a thick, black liquid oozes out of the man's ass and runs down the woman's rolls. The big lady acts as if she doesn't notice anything happening and Sandra wonders if she's asleep. The woman moves slightly and her rolls jiggle. Sandra can see the calloused flesh in between the rolls, along with dark red sores lining creases of her skin. The doctor pulls his face away from the woman's large red areola and Sandra sees a dark brown liquid streaming out of her nipple and running down the corner of his mouth. Even from her distance, Sandra can smell the vile stench of whatever disgusting milk the woman is producing. She turns back into the main room and gags.

"Is someone there?" Leningrad asks. He steps off of the mother cow, sliding through the black ooze of his feces, and takes two steps toward the main room, making shit footprints as he walks. "You need to be out wrangling in the bull, it's all hands out in the fields right now."

Sandra looks around the dark room, trying to find a weapon of some kind. She's naked and feels vulnerable, unsure of what to do if he attacks her.

"Hello? Is anyone out there?" he asks again, and Sandra can tell he is getting closer. She could run, she's certain she can make it to the door before he saw her, but she can't help thinking this man could show her the truth about her baby. She wants to see with her own eyes what they do to the babies born here, she wants to know for sure that it is over.

When Leningrad turns the corner into the main room Sandra can't help letting a little gasp escape. His naked, sagging body is half covered in black shit and brown milk, the smell wafting from him is foul, and his cock is hard, though just a tiny nub pointing out from his pelvis. His eyes, which she remembers being covered by dark glasses before, are wide and wild. He looks like a crazy man, and Sandra questions the decision she made to stay and face him.

“A cow? What are you doing here? Why are you standing, cows don’t stand,” Leningrad says. He stands there in the doorway to the back room appraising her. “Get to your knees as you belong. I will escort you back to your stall. This is unacceptable.”

He begins walking toward her and Sandra feels the panic start to set in. She can hear his feet slapping the floor and his deep breathing, and her heart pounding in her chest. She takes a quick look to the left and then the right, there is just nothing in the room she can use to defend herself. He's on her before she can react. Leningrad knocks her down, his saggy body on top of her, pinning her to the floor.

"I remember you, you're one of the new cows," he says, his face an inch away from hers, his foul breath assaulting her even more than the odor from the fluids on his body, She retches, afraid she might throw up lying there on her back and start choking on her own vomit. "If I remember correctly, they were having trouble breaking you. I'm guessing you're still resisting, seeing as how you are here where you don't belong. Why don't you moo for me cow, maybe I'll go easy on you."

Sandra struggles underneath him but he's too heavy, his grip on her wrists too strong. She spits at his face, her only defense at this point. A glob of saliva hits him on the cheek and he smiles. He pushes a thick tongue out and licks at his cheek, trying to get at her spit on his face.

"I like them feisty; I don't like a cow that

just lays there and takes it," he says. He lets go of one of her wrists and reaches between her legs.

"What is this?" he says, pulling his hand back with some meat on his finger. He looks at it in confusion and then looks up at Sandra. She doesn't hesitate and reaches out and shoves her thumb into his eye. She feels the orb deform under the pressure of her thumb and Leningrad screams out. He lets go of her and rolls off, one hand going up to his injured eyeball. Sandra sits up as her stomach muscles burn in protest. She stands and quickly moves over to Leningrad, who has one hand over his injured eye. He looks up at her with his good eye just as she stomps down on his tiny, but still erect, penis, the heel of her foot smashing his shaft and his balls into his pelvis.

Sandra doesn't let up and smashes her foot into his cock over and over. Leningrad covers his junk, but she continues to stomp with the heel of her foot and smashes it into his hands. He turns away from Sandra, her foot in the air ready for one more strike, and vomits a dark, thick liquid onto the floor next to him. She puts her foot back down to the floor gently, it hurts now but she can manage.

"I'm not a cow you rapist, murdering piece of shit," she spits at him vehemently. "I will never moo for you fucking scum, I will die before I ever fucking moo."

He lays there on his side moaning as blood runs from his urethra. Sandra doubts that he will be able to tell her much now, so she walks away from him and into the back room. The mother cow sits breathing heavily. The dark brown liquid is still seeping from her nipple and disappearing into the folds of her massive flesh.

The mother cow opens her sad eyes to look at Sandra. Her lips crack as they move around the tube in her mouth, but if she's trying to say something, Sandra can't hear it. But she thinks he understands all the same. The sad eyes, now with tears trickling down the sides tell her everything she needs to know.

Sandra follows the tubes across the ceiling to the machines they are connected to. There's a multitude of lights and switches, but she instantly sees one that stands out as possibly the disconnect. Sandra wraps her hand around the handle and pulls the lever down. All the lights blink out in unison and the machines go quiet. The room is filled with only the loud, harsh breathing of the mother cow. Sandra turns back to her, she's wheezing, and her breath is labored. She wonders how long it's been since the woman tried to breathe on her own. There's a slight movement of the large women's head that Sandra understands is the only thanks she can give her. Sandra nods back and leaves the big lady to die in peace.

Back in the main room, she sees Leningrad is gone.

# Chapter 9

Sandra walks down past the door of the delivery room and can see outside through an open bay door fifty yards away. It's bright out, and she can see the short green grass of a field. Off to the right she sees a fence, it's tall and the barbed wire across the top of it gleams in the sunlight. She imagines that is the pens the bulls are kept in. There's no way she can go out that door without being spotted. There is a really good chance George and his cronies will be out there. She is naked and completely defenseless. Somewhere there is a fire, she can smell it. Shitheel must have been telling the truth she thinks, he really is going to burn this place down.

Thinking maybe she should just save herself, run from this place, and not look back, Sandra turns to make her way going the opposite direction of the bull's pens. She quickly moves around the corner from the delivery room door and finds herself walking through a series of corridors constructed with similar wood to the stalls they keep the woman in. Sandra does not like this, she feels trapped, and her only options are to keep pushing forward or turn around and try to find another way. She stops, weighing her options when she hears something behind her. She looks back, trying to listen, but she can't tell what it is, and she doesn't see anything yet. Regardless, this fixes her conundrum, she has to keep pushing forward.

The corridor goes on for what feels like an eternity to Sandra, every time she thinks she's reached an exit it's just an extension jutting off in a different direction. It feels like she is being led somewhere, and she's scared of where she is going to end up.

The soles of Sandra's bare feet hurt. Before whatever all of this is happened to her, she didn't spend much time walking around without shoes on. Her feet were soft and unaccustomed to the abuse they are receiving as she wandered around the facility. When she finally turns the corner that leads her to the end of this maze, she wants to be grateful, but there's a pretty intense smell. It is a rotten smell, like spoiled meat that has sat out for too long.

In the middle of an open area sits a big machine. It is off, but it looks well-used. Oil can be seen on the casing as if it leaks while its running, and the ground underneath is stained black. Walking toward it, she wonders what it is and what it is used for. When she is close to it she reaches a hand out and feels the heat rising off of it. She walks around to the front side of it and sees a troth with slimy meat chunks down in the corners that looks an awful lot like the meat they forced her to eat.

She brings her hand to her nose, this is where the smell is coming from, and being this close to it is nauseating.

Sandra moves away from the machine, she has a pretty good idea what it is, and she can't fight back the tears that began to run down her cheeks. Keeping her eyes on it like she expects it to burst into life and begin grinding up little babies right in front of her, she backs away from the machine. Someone grabs her from behind and she lets out a shriek.

"How the fuck did you get out?" George asks as he lifts Sandra off her feet and tosses her to the ground. The impact is hard and knocks the wind out of her. "After all this time you still haven't learned your place."

She looks up at George's hulking person as he steps toward her. Behind him is a large group of farmers dressed just like George. The exception is the naked Leningrad.

"She killed the mother cow!" Leningrad yells accusatorily. He is just as naked as she left him, his balls and tiny cock were bruised and red. She would have thought it was ridiculous, but the mob in front of her froze her in fear.

"Grab her boys, we need to bring the mother cow back from the dead to keep the bowery alive," George says. The mob surges forward and Sandra tries to fight but it's absurd really. Dozens of hands grab onto her naked flesh, and they pick her up from the dirt floor and raise her high into the air. The hands touch all over her entire body. Groping her breasts and ass, fingers enter her pussy and asshole, her nostrils, and her mouth. She swings her arms and legs as she tries to knock the hands and probing fingers away.

The mob of people takes her back into the maze-like corridor. There are so many bodies they fill almost every inch of the small corridor as she is carried through. The hands holding her up change constantly like they are moving her along from person to person. The fear of being dropped is palpable, but it never happens, she is only pulled down just to a couple of feet above the dirt floor when they reach the door that will take them to the mother cow.

Sandra can see George pull the door open as the naked Leningrad leads the mob into the main room and through to the back where the still-warm corpse of the obese lady is. Sandra's feet are sat down on the floor, but she is still held by her arms and around her neck. She is squeezed so tight her vision darkens at the edges, and breathing is difficult. But she stands there and watches as men move to the mother cow. They grab a large fat roll and lift it high into the air, displaying the rough, sore speckled skin underneath. The big woman's skin is red and calloused, and when it's stretched it breaks open and thick pus oozes out. The smell seeps into Sandra's nostrils but she appears to be the only person in the room affected by it.

George walks past her and she sees the long knife in his hand, hanging nonchalantly at his side. He steps up to where the men hold the fat roll in the air, the skin now shiny and wet from the pus. George lifts the knife and slices the skin open, the flesh peeling back easily under the sharp blade. He cuts her open from one side to the other, and the wet and slimy insides of the mother cow spill out at her bare and swollen feet.

Watching this makes Sandra's stomach turn. She can feel the saliva building in her mouth as a precursor to vomiting, but before she can even begin to retch, she is lifted off of her feet and carried toward the mother cow. George turns and looks her in the eyes as the men lift her into the open body cavity of the obese woman. Sandra can't even attempt to fight; they hold her so tightly. They shove her into the bloody viscera that is left in the corpse and lower the fat roll back in place, sealing Sandra in.

# Chapter 10

Sandra is surprised to not be suffocating inside the body of the big lady. She knows enough about basic human anatomy to know that she should be surrounded by all the digestive organs that reside in one's stomach cavity and that there definitely should not be room enough for a fully grown woman to comfortably fit. But, instead of being anything that Sandra thought it would be, she feels more like she is inside a deprivation tank.

Her body floats in a vast nothingness, no part of her flesh touches anything. There is no light and no sound, she feels completely cut off from all sensations. How is this possible, she wonders. Did she pass out from lack of oxygen inside the cooling corpse of the big woman? Is this all a dream her mind is conjuring up as her body slowly shut down on her way to becoming a corpse inside of a corpse?

Suddenly, Sandra knows there is another presence. She tries to look around but still, there is nothing. Is her head even turning when she tells it to?

But there is someone, or rather, something. It nudges at her mind, not her body, like it is trying to push her out of the way. It's comforting, like a warm embrace around her brain. It reminds her of a really good pill high, the warmth that would fill her body, and the numbness that she so loved back then. She had given all that up when she became pregnant, the baby was going to be her life, not the partying and everything else she used to do.

But the feeling comes back so easily and quickly, Sandra just wants to lie back and let it envelop her. She can just float away, her insides feeling warm and comforted, she can forget about the hell she has been put through since she's been here. She can forget about her baby, her dead baby, gone but still inside her, she saw to that. She'll keep that baby inside her forever now, it will always be a part of her.

Sandra can't feel her face, but she knows she is smiling. This is the release she looked for most of her life. This is the peace she never knew was possible.

Sandra's mind begins to shut down as the mother cow takes hold. She does not know what is happening to her, her brain is filling with endorphins and making her comfortable and happy with the transformation that she will undergo. Every fiber of her being begins to stretch out and touch every piece of the mother cow, a connection is forming, and she is losing herself to the point that there will be no more Sandra, only the mother cow.

Then, she feels a searing, tearing sensation she has never felt before. It makes her want to curl up into a little ball and pull into herself so that she is in a defensive position. A pain, unlike any other rips through her brain. Something is screaming, is it her? No, something else is screaming that was almost her. She is being separated from the mother cow just as quickly as she was joining. But she was joined enough that she feels that disconnection tremendously, and it does not feel good.

Everything around her closes in, she is smashed between thick ropey organs and something heavy and wet. Sandra can't breathe, she really is suffocating inside a corpse. She is covered in black slime and as she tries to breathe in the smell penetrates her sinuses and she begins to retch. She gags and the black slime fills her mouth. She tries to spit it out but there's so much, there isn't anywhere for it to go.

Something grabs her ankle, and her leg is yanked. It hurts, another pull, and she thinks her leg is going to be ripped off. Another pull and her whole body moves. She pushes her hands into a thin sac of something that explodes against the force, but she moves.

Sandra slams onto the floor in a dimly lit room and coughs and gags, black slime drooling from her lips. She wipes gunk from her eyes trying to see what is happening. Shitheel is kneeling in front of her, his hands covered in the same black slime.

"I don't know how to explain what was happening," Sandra says, looking behind her to the corpse of the mother cow.

"If you would have stayed in there too long, you would have become the new mother cow," Shitheel says. He wipes his hands on his overalls making black streaks down the length of his clothing.

"Thank you for saving me," Sandra says.

"I'm trying to burn this place down, I can't let them create a new mother cow," Shitheel says. "Come on, we need to go now. They'll be back soon to check on you and make sure the process takes hold."

Sandra lifts herself to a standing position and looks down at her naked body covered in drying and hardening black crap. She sees

Shitheel disappear around the corner and takes off after him.

Shitheel walks carefully along the stalls, trying to keep an eye out for any of the farmers that would try to stop them from escaping. It would be easy enough to blend in with his fellow workers until he reaches a point where he can run, but having Sandra with him is making things a little trickier.

As they walk, women moo at them or just to themselves. Shitheel pays them no mind, but Sandra feels sorry for the women. She still wants to help them, not just abandon them here to continue being assaulted and abused by the twisted people that work there. The only option she feels like she has at this point is to get out and get to the authorities to get them to go back to the place.

They walk past Sandra's stall, sitting wide open. She wants to avoid it, and walk as far around it as she can, but she ignores those feelings and keeps herself pressed close just as she has been doing. As Shitheel walks past the open stall door George comes barreling out of the stall and grabs Shitheel by the throat.

"What the fuck are you doing, boy?" George asks as he slams Shitheel into a solid wooden wall. The farmer turns his head and looks at Sandra, then looks back to Shitheel. "I knew something wasn't right with you, and here you are, with our mother cow. Where do you think you're taking her?"

Shitheel can't speak from George's huge hand crushing his throat. The bigger man's question seems rhetorical anyway. George produced a knife from somewhere in his overalls and stabs Shitheel in his side. Shitheel kicks his legs and fights against George's grip, but he isn't strong enough to fight him off. George quickly stabs the younger man three more times in the same side and then drops him to the dirt. Shitheel lands hard and crumbles onto the ground. George whirls on Sandra faster than she would have expected a man of his size to and shoves her to the ground.

"Your time here isn't up yet cow," George

says, slipping the bloody knife back into his overalls pocket.

“We have plans for you, you are going to be a special heifer for us, our mother cow.”

Sandra tries to crawl away from him as he walks toward her. George lifts one heavy boot and kicks her on her ass. She screams out in pain and falls flat on her stomach, the impact inflaming the pain of her c-section scar.

“You are not getting out of here, cow. You never mooed for me,” he says. Sandra looks over her shoulder at the man and sees that he is unhooking the straps of his overalls. “Before you go back to the mother cow, I think you're going to have to moo for me.”

Sandra gets back on her hands and knees to start crawling again and George reaches down and grabs one of her ankles and pulls her backward. She falls flat again, but George doesn’t let up and drags her across the dirt floor. She throws her hands out, trying for purchase on the dirt but it just comes up as her fingers dig into it. She sees Shitheel’s body on the ground, blood pouring from him, and soaking into the dirt. George drags her into the open stall and Sandra flips out, screaming and kicking at the man. He lets go of her leg and she gets up trying to get her feet under her to run out of the stall, but big, calloused hands grab her around her waist. The world spins out of control as George lifts her into the air and slams her into the ground. The impact is hard, and she feels something pop in her shoulder. Sandra is dazed but she still tries to crawl away, only now she's turned around, crawling further into the back of the stall.

"Now, this will be your last breeding before you become the mother cow, then the breeding's will be slightly different," George says as he unhooks his overalls the rest of the way and lets them drop to the ground. Sandra looks over her shoulder and can see him there, completely naked, his cock thick and hard. "You're going to moo for me this time, or else I'm not going to be as easy on you as I've been before. You can still be the mother cow with some broken bones and a broken jaw."

George reaches down and grabs both of Sandra's ankles and pulls her towards him. Straw digs into her flesh as he drags her across the ground. She tries to fight him off as he practically falls on top of her. George pushes her legs forward like he's trying to fold her in half. She can feel the wet head of his cock touching her, trying to find the entrance into her warm center. Then, George's head is pulled backward like he decided to stare up at the ceiling. He's twisted away to her right, and then he falls forward.

Despite being confused about what is happening, Sandra manages to pull her leg out of the way before George is pushed to the ground next to her. She looks up and sees the bull from before, the one she watched assault another girl and hurt her badly.

"What in the fuck?" George says as he tries to twist out of the bull's grip. The bull looks at Sandra, he's as naked as she is, as George is. But the bull has an erect cock that puts George's to shame. Being this close to it scares her. She's seen the damage that thing can cause, and as it throbs and leaks pre-cum, she isn't sure what this creature is intending to do with it.

The bull turns its attention back to the man wriggling to be free in front of him. He pushes George's head to the ground and brings his engorged dick up to his ass, wedging it in between his two flabby ass cheeks, and pushes. Women in stalls on either side of the one they're in moo loudly and bang into the wooden slats almost as if they're cheering the bull on.

"Hey, get off me! What the fuck do you think you're doing!" George says before he begins to scream. Sandra watches as the farmer's asshole is spread open by the huge purple head forcing its way inside. She sees the flesh around his rectum begin to split and she decides she doesn't want to see anymore. She is on her feet and out of the stall fast.

There's no more sneaking around the stalls trying not to get caught, Sandra is flat-out running. Her feet hit the floor hard, and she ignores every bit of pain that comes from it. The same with her throbbing shoulder, it's all irrelevant to her as she sprints towards what she hopes is freedom.

# Chapter 11

The fires Shitheel started burn through an unused portion of the bowery. His intention was to set ablaze an area no one frequented so that the flames would have time to sufficiently tear into the wooden beams and supports. He had hoped that once it got its hold there, it would quickly spread through the rest of the place, consuming everything in its path. Unfortunately for Shitheel, the fire is spotted earlier than he had anticipated and all the men that had gathered together to search for the escaped bull and subsequently found Sandra running free are able to attack the fire and get it under control before it does any real damage to the structure at all.

After the fires are dealt with, Shitheel's body is found, along with George. It isn't difficult for the farmers to figure out what happened since Sandra is also missing. The men string up the corpse of Shitheel and hang him above the big door leading out to the fields as a reminder to anyone of what will happen if they attempted an escape.

All this time, Sandra is running. She rans across fields, spends a freezing cold night lost in the woods, and makes her way to some semblance of civilization. She finds clothes to wear on another farms, a real farms, clothesline. Sandra is then able to convince a farmer to drive her into the nearest town so that she can talk to the police. She guves her statement, tells them everything that had happened, and they take her to their local hospital with promises to investigate her claims.

Sandra never hears from the police again. Two deputies do find the farm after an exhausting search all over the county. They are taken in, shown around, and captured. The two deputies are then forced into the bull's pen and die horrible deaths.

Once she feels well enough to leave the hospital, Sandra disappears too. She is paranoid about how she had been taken to the farm. She has no memory of how they kidnapped her, or where from. She spends every moment in the hospital thinking they will find her. The first opportunity she has, she runs again. She goes home and spends every day looking over her shoulder.

# Chapter 12

The sound of a baby crying wakes Sandra. That wasn't anything new, it is actually a frequent occurrence. She dreams about the son she did not have and has nightmares about the place that took him away. She gets up from her bed and makes her way to her kitchen to get a drink of something to wash away the bad dreams. The house is dark as she makes her way through it, keeping the lights off in the hope that she'll have an easier time falling back asleep.

Opening the refrigerator blinds her momentarily. She grabs for a bottle of water, finds her prize, and steps away from the appliance. She sets the water down on the counter and grips the edge. Her paranoia is going nuts tonight.

Sandra walks away from the counter, forgetting all about her water. She traces her steps taking her back to her bedroom but stops in the hallway. Her breathing becomes ragged, her heart beat intensifies.

Slowly she turns her head to look into her living room and she sees what she fears will be there. The silhouette of a big man.

“Hello cow,” Steph says from the darkness.

Sandra bolts down the hallway. The only thought in her mind is her gun, a Taurus .45 in the nightstand beside her table.

In the darkness of the hallway she can’t see the giant wall of a man that steps out of her bedroom. Sandra slams into him and crashes to the floor.

“We’ve been looking for you, cow,” Steph says from behind her. “We need our mother cow back to keep the farm running.”

Sandra lifts her self up on her elbows. She

has spent so long worrying that this day would come. She can't believe that it is here now, and she isn't better prepared. Memories of what they did to her come flooding back into her mind. She can’t do that again, she won’t do that again.

“I won’t go back, I’ll kill myself before I let you fucking rapists touch me again,” Sandra says to Steph, but not taking her eyes off the big man standing over her.

“Yeah, kinda figured you weren’t gonna come easy,” Steph says. He turns his head back toward the living room. “Seth! Bring it in!”

Sandra hears the crying before anything else. She lifts herself from the floor, the big man taking a step back to give her space. The crying continues and Sandra can feel the tears streaming down her face. She walks back toward the living room, pushing past Steph. A boy, not much older than Shitheel was and dressed the same, stands there holding a crying baby.

“We usually destroy the calves, but George thought we should keep yours alive. He knew you were something special, and he was right. You're the new mother cow," Steph says to her as she walks toward the boy holding the baby. "If you come with us, you can have him back."

Sandra turns and looks at Steph, her mind reeling with emotions. She turns back and looks at the baby, her baby, and raises her arms to take the child.

## ABOUT THE AUTHOR

Matthew Vaughn is the author of The ADHD Vampire, Mother Fucking Black Skull of Death, Hellsworld Hotel, and 30 Minutes or Less. With his brother, Edward Vaughn, they edited and compiled The Classics Never Die! An Anthology of Old School Movie Monsters for their own press, Red All Over Books.
He lives in Shelbyville, Kentucky and is the father of five kids, yet he and his wife are just big kids too. By day he maintains machines and robots, by night he is a writer of Bizarro and Horror fiction. You can keep up with his work at:

http://authormatthewvaughn.com/

https://www.facebook.com/

AuthorMatthewVaughn

https://twitter.com/mcvaughn138

**https://www.instagram.com/**
**m_f_n_black_skull_of_death**

Made in United States
Troutdale, OR
12/12/2023